peg + cat

PEG UP A TREE

A LEVEL 1 READER

JENNIFER OXLEY
+ BILLY ARONSON

CANDLEWICK
ENTERTAINMENT

Up in a Tree

Peg has a BIG PROBLEM!
She is stuck up in a tree.
Cat is down on the ground.
Peg doesn't see
that Cat is there.
Cat doesn't see
that Peg is there.

Peg sings:
"Being stuck in a tree
is not for me!
La-dee-dee!"

Peg plays with her yo-yo.
She swings it up.

She swings it down.

BONK!

The yo-yo hits Cat on the head.

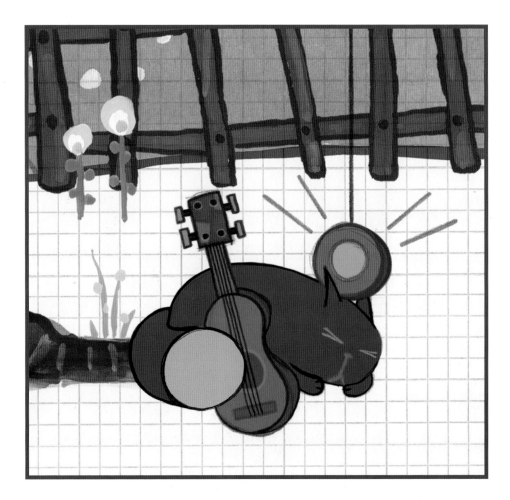

"Peg!" says Cat. "Are
you stuck in a tree?"

"Cat!" says Peg. "I'm so
glad you found me! Can you
help me get down?"

"You can count on me,"
says Cat.

Down on the Ground

"Peg always helps me," says
Cat. "Now I can help her."
  Cat thinks. He rolls.
He sniffs a flower. He
sneezes. ACHOO!

  The flower breaks. The
parts look like a ladder.
"I will build a big ladder
to get Peg down," says Cat.

Cat finds two long poles and five little pieces of wood.

He gets a jump rope.

He ties the poles and wood together.

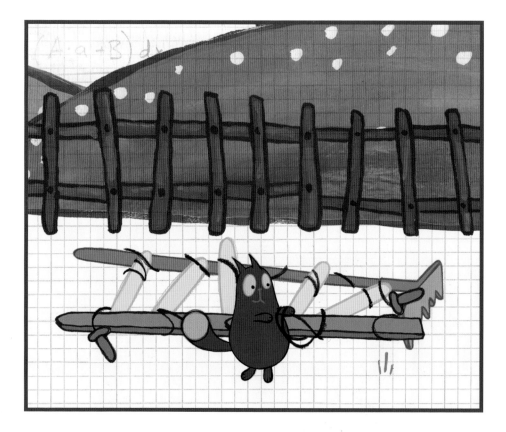

"Peg!" says Cat. "I will go up this ladder to get you down!"

"That is a ladder?" asks Peg.

"I made it myself!" says Cat.

Cat goes up the ladder.

He slides to
the right.
"Whoa!"

He slides to
the left.
"Yaaa!"

The ladder falls!

"NOOOO!"

Peg grabs Cat.

Now both Peg and Cat are stuck in the tree! They have a REALLY BIG PROBLEM!

Up, Down, and All Around

"Hey, Peg and Cat!" says
Ramone. "What are you doing
up in the tree?"

"We are trying to get
down," says Peg.

"But our ladder does not
work," says Cat.

"The sides need to go up
and down," says Ramone.
"And the steps need to go
across."

Ramone fixes the ladder so the sides and steps are just right.

"I will go up this ladder to get you down," says Ramone.

Peg cheers. "WOO HOO!"
Cat jumps for joy!

Cat's jump makes
the ladder fall!
Ramone grabs on
to a branch, and Peg
helps pull him up.

Now all three are stuck
in the tree!

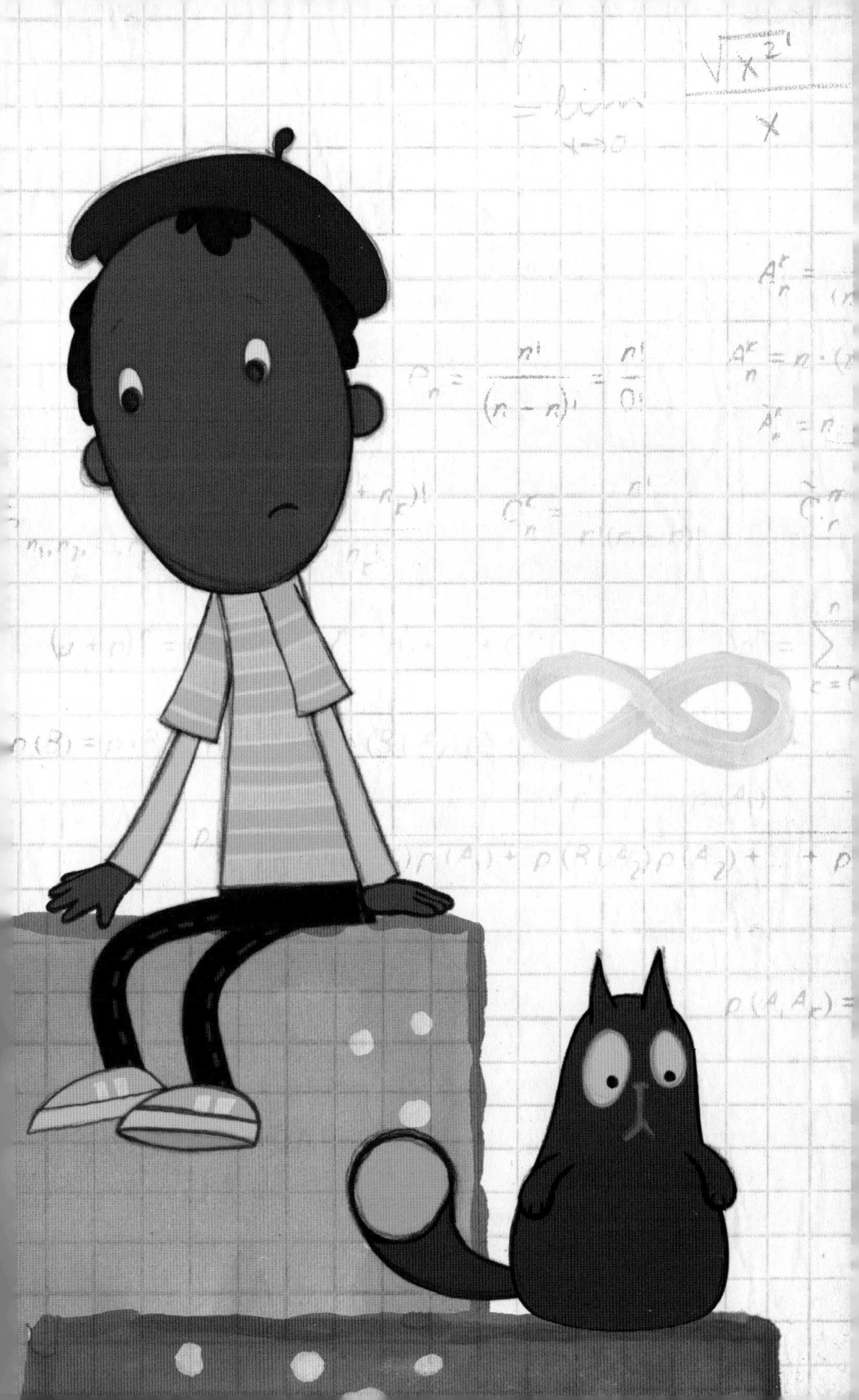

Peg looks at Cat's tail.
It looks like a yo-yo.

"Yes!" says Peg. "I can use my yo-yo to get us down."

Peg swings her yo-yo down.
The yo-yo grabs the ladder.
Peg pulls the ladder up.

"You are good with that yo-yo," says Ramone.

"Thanks, Ramone!" says Peg.

Ramone climbs down. Cat
climbs down. Peg climbs
down.

Now no one is stuck up
in the tree.

Problem solved!

This book is based on the TV series *Peg + Cat*.
Peg + Cat is produced by Fred Rogers Productions.
Peg Up a Tree is based on a TV script by Jennifer Oxley.
Art assets assembled by Erica Kepler.
The PBS KIDS logo is a registered mark of the Public
Broadcasting Service and is used with permission.

pbskids.org/peg

First edition 2019

Library of Congress Catalog Card Number pending
ISBN 978-1-5362-0968-6 (hardcover)
ISBN 978-1-5362-0970-9 (paperback)

19 20 21 22 23 24 APS 10 9 8 7 6 5 4 3 2 1

Printed in Humen, Dongguan, China

This book was typeset in OPTITypewriter.
The illustrations were created digitally.

Candlewick Entertainment
an imprint of Candlewick Press
99 Dover Street
Somerville, Massachusetts 02144

visit us at www.candlewick.com